Acting Edition

Today Is My Birthday

by Susan Soon He Stanton

FOR PRODUCTION INQUIRIES

UNITED STATES AND CANADA
info@concordtheatricals.com
1-866-979-0447

UNITED KINGDOM AND EUROPE
licensing@concordtheatricals.co.uk
020-7054-7298

Each title is subject to availability from Concord Theatricals Corp.,
depending upon country of performance. Please be aware that *TODAY
IS MY BIRTHDAY* may not be licensed by Concord Theatricals Corp.
in your territory. Professional and amateur producers should contact
the nearest Concord Theatricals Corp. office or licensing partner to
verify availability.

MUSIC AND THIRD-PARTY MATERIALS USE NOTE

Licensees are solely responsible for obtaining formal written permission from copyright owners to use copyrighted music and/or other copyrighted third-party materials (e.g., artworks, logos) in the performance of this play and are strongly cautioned to do so. If no such permission is obtained by the licensee, then the licensee must use only original music and materials that the licensee owns and controls. Licensees are solely responsible and liable for clearances of all third-party copyrighted materials, including without limitation music, and shall indemnify the copyright owners of the play(s) and their licensing agent, Concord Theatricals Corp., against any costs, expenses, losses and liabilities arising from the use of such copyrighted third-party materials by licensees. For music, please contact the appropriate music licensing authority in your territory for the rights to any incidental music.

IMPORTANT BILLING AND CREDIT REQUIREMENTS

If you have obtained performance rights to this title, please refer to your licensing agreement for important billing and credit requirements.

TODAY IS MY BIRTHDAY was developed at Sundance Theater Lab, New York Theater Workshop, American Conservatory Theater, and New York Stage & Film with the Lark. In 2017, *Today Is My Birthday* won the Venturous Theater Award for best New Play, The Kilroy's List, and received a Susan Smith Blackburn nomination. This play was produced by Page 73 in November 2017, directed by Kip Fagan. The cast was as follows:

EMILY . . . . .Jennifer Ikeda
MOM . . . . Emily Kuroda
DAD/BILL TAPIA . . . . Ron Domingo
FRANKLIN & OTHERS . . . . Ugo Chukwu
DJ LOKI/LANDON & OTHERS . . . . Jonathan Brooks
HALIMA . . . . Nadine Malouf

CREATIVE TEAM

Dane Laffrey | Set Design
Jessica Pabst | Costume Design
Jen Schriever | Lighting Design
Palmer Hefferan | Sound Design/Live Foley Artist
Alison Mantilla | Prop Design
Kara Kaufman | Production Stage Manager
Justin Myhre | Assistant Stage Manager
Intuitive Prod. Mgmt. | Production Management
Carly D. Shiner | Assistant. Lighting
Nok Kanchanabanca | Assistant Sound
Sinan Zafar | Assistant Sound
Liz Frino | Assistant Props
Caterina Nonis | Assistant Director
Maya Eilam | Graphic Design

TODAY IS MY BIRTHDAY was performed at Yale Repertory Theatre in January 2022, directed by Mina Morita. The cast was as follows:

EMILY . . . . Jeena Yi
MOM/MRS. KOBAYASHI/ALYSSA/JOYCE/MRS. ASUNCION/ PATSY . . . . Emily Kuroda
DAD/BILL TAPIA . . . . Francis Jue
KURT/RICHARD/SEBASTIAN/KEONI/SERGIO/FRANKLIN . . . .
. . . . Gabriel Brown

DJ LOKI/GRANDPA Z/ DR. JOHANNNES CONNECTION/ LANDON/ AMAZINGPRESENCE83/TROY .... Chivas Michael

HALIMA/DJ SOLANGE/GODDESS SWEET LEILANI/HOSTESS/ GENERIC FEMALE VOICE .... Atra Asdou

CREATIVE TEAM

Bridget Lindsay | Set Designer

David Mitsch | Costume Designer

Nicole E. Lang | Lighting Designer

Noel Nichols | Sound Designer

Matthew Armentrout | Hair Designer

Jisun Kim | Production Dramaturg

Dani Mader | Technical Director

Cynthia Santos DeCure | Vocal and Dialect Coach

Erica Fae | Movement Coach

Tara Rubin, C.S.A. | Casting Director

Sujotta Pace, C.S.A. | Casting Director

Kevin Jinghong Zhu | Stage Manager

This production is part of the Lark's Venturous Playwright Fellowship Program, funded by Venturous Theater Fund of the Tides Foundation.

Today Is My Birthday is supported in part by the New York State Council on the arts with the support of governor Andrew M. Cuomo and the New York State Legislate.

CHARACTERS

EMILY – a temp

(All other roles should be doubled as much as possible.)

POSSIBLE DOUBLINGS

MOM – Emily's Mother

MRS. KOBAYASHI – Receptionist

ALYSSA – Bill Tapia's manager

JOYCE – Public radio hostess

MRS. ASUNCION – Landon's mother and editor for newspaper

DAD – Emily's Father

BILL TAPIA – 103-year-old ukulele player, world's oldest performing musician

KURT – Artistic Director of Hawai'i Repertory Theatre

RICHARD – Emily's Boss

SEBASTIAN – Emily's ex-boyfriend

KEONI/JONATHAN/FRANKLIN – Emily's on-air love interest

DJ LOKI – FM DJ

GRANDPA Z – Caricature grandpa performed by DJ Loki

DR. JOHANNNES CONNECTION – German Radio Shrink performed by DJ Loki

LANDON – Emily's high school friend

AMAZINGPRESENCE83 – A phone helpline volunteer

TROY – Emily's ex-boyfriend

HALIMA – Emily's best friend

DJ SOLANGE – FM DJ

GODDESS SWEET LEILANI – ADVICE Guru performed by DJ Solange

HOSTESS – Works at Doraku Restaurant

GENERIC FEMALE VOICE

SETTING

Primarily set in Honolulu on Oahu Island, Hawai'i and in New York City.

TIME

The events of this play are loosely set in mid-2015.

AUTHOR'S NOTES

This is a play that entirely takes place on the telephone, live radio, voice message, and intercom. No characters are in the same physical location as Emily. Doubling is highly encouraged as much as possible.

This play, while relying on technology which constantly changes, shouldn't feel like a period piece. If the reference to Facebook feels too dated, the following lines can be cut:

HALIMA. He's not my friend.

~~**EMILY.** But he's your Facebook friend.~~

~~**HALIMA.** I unfriended him when you two broke up.~~

EMILY. Halima, why would you do that? How am I going to / know–?

HALIMA. I'm a mother of two, I can't stalk your ex-boyfriends for you.

MUSIC NOTES

I strongly encourage the creative team to listen to morning talk radio programs and specifically Honolulu Radio Stations. The music is a blend of modern Hawaiian, Jawaiian, and contemporary American top 100. There are also a number of stingers liberally applied to these programs.

One

(Telephone rings.)

EMILY. Hello?

KURT. Hey, Emily.

EMILY. Hey Kurt! We're still on for lunch? Noon right?

KURT. Shit.

EMILY. It's okay.

KURT. Sorreeee. So I got a question for you.

EMILY. Shoot.

KURT. So Honolulu Repertory Theater gets free advertising from a radio station. But they need actors to call in and respond to various scenarios.

EMILY. So there are fake people who call in?

KURT. Oh yeah. No actual people call radio stations.

EMILY. That's so disappointing.

KURT. If you're in, I'll email you the scenario and they'll call you tomorrow morning. It's basic improv.

EMILY. Kurt, I'm not an actor.

KURT. Andrea dropped out and I'm stuck.

EMILY. Can't you do it? Or find an actual actor?

KURT. They need a woman. I'm in a bind. It'll be fun!

EMILY. It's just, I've never acted before. And public speaking...

KURT. Don't worry about it. It was a long shot. Hold on – Hi. Flat white. Extra hot. Oat milk.

EMILY. You know what, I'm in. What the hell.

KURT. Really?

EMILY. Why, are you surprised I'm doing it?

KURT. Kinda. Thanks!

(Click.)

Two

(Telephone rings.)

MOM. Chang Residence. You've reached Grace.

EMILY. That's how you answer the phone now?

MOM. Who is this???

EMILY. Your daughter.

MOM. Mimi??

EMILY. Mom, you just called me.

MOM. Did you get the article I sent you?

EMILY. Hold on.

(Letter opening.)

MOM. Why do I mail you these things if you don't read them?

EMILY. *(Reading.)* Thirty is NOT the new twenty: Top psychologist says twenty-somethings are damaging future career and relationships by treating the decade as 'downtime' before real life begins.

MOM. Go on.

EMILY. This idea causes twenty-somethings to become passive, believing they have plenty of time to build their careers and find love later in life.

MOM. I mail you these clippings to inspire you. So you don't rest on your laurels.

EMILY. What laurels?

MOM. Exactly.

Now honey. Did any of the magazines or newspapers respond to your articles?

EMILY. Well. You know sometimes it takes a few pitches to get people interested.

MOM. I thought you were going to do that blob you wanted to make.

EMILY. It's called a blog. And my digital magazine's not ready.

MOM. How will it ever be ready if you –

EMILY. MOM. If you want, you can listen to Z 101.3 tomorrow morning. I'll be on the radio.

MOM. You're doing a piece for the radio!?!

EMILY. Sort of. On Z 101.3, you can nominate a hot guy at your job to be the Office Stud of the Week. I'm pretending to be a woman named Iris. I hear his voice and fall in love with him. And I call the radio station to see if he wants to hook up.

MOM. I don't understand.

EMILY. It's acting.

MOM. It's demeaning to ask out a boy on the radio.

EMILY. I'm Meg Ryan in *Sleepless in Seattle*.

MOM. You should call your father.

EMILY. About this?

MOM. Do you need a reason to call your father?

EMILY. Is something wrong?

MOM. Call your father sweetie. Don't make me ask you again.

　　　　(Click.)

Three

(Telephone rings. **MRS. KOBAYASHI** *is sharpening pencils.)*

MRS. KOBAYASHI. CDF Solutions. How may I direct your call?

EMILY. Hello Mrs. Kobayashi, this is Emily.

MRS. KOBAYASHI. And how may I help you, Emily?

EMILY. No. Oh. I work there?

MRS. KOBAYASHI. I'm so sorry. How is it that we haven't met?

EMILY. I'm replacing Trisha on her maternity leave.

MRS. KOBAYASHI. *(Less sweet.)* You're the temp.

EMILY. Yes. I was just calling to let Richard know that I might be fifteen minutes late.

MRS. KOBAYASHI. I will put a note on *Mr. Hall's* desk. Shall I indicate a reason why you will be late?

EMILY. It's just that, I'm going to be interviewed on the radio. And it's not safe to talk and drive on the phone. It's illegal? So I'll be getting a late start.

MRS. KOBAYASHI. What station? I have a radio right here on my desk, we can tune in.

EMILY. I rather not say, if you don't mind. It's nothing bad. You'll let Richard - Mr. Hall, I mean, you'll let him know?

MRS. KOBAYASHI. Mmhmm.

EMILY. Thanks.

You're there really early. I was just going to transfer to his voicemail.

MRS. KOBAYASHI. I'm always here early. Would you *prefer* me to transfer you to his voicemail?

EMILY. No, a note's fine.

Well. Uh. I'll be on Z 101.3 at eight thirty a.m. But I'll be answering under the name Iris.

If you want to listen in…

MRS. KOBAYASHI. That's okay, Emily. We will see you later.

(Click.)

Four

(Telephone rings.)

HALIMA. Hey girl.

EMILY. Hey Halima.

HALIMA. I missed it, didn't I?

EMILY. No, I'm going on in thirty minutes! I'm just calling because I'm nervous.

I'm not like, a *performer*, you know?

HALIMA. You'll be great. This is so great you are doing this.

It's great.

You're finally settling back in Hawaii.

EMILY. Not really. I have too much proximity to my upbringing.

HALIMA. New York misses you.

EMILY. I miss New York.

HALIMA. But not Sebastian?

EMILY. Hell no.

HALIMA. Good.

EMILY. Does he know I moved?

HALIMA. He's not my friend.

EMILY. But he's your Facebook friend.

HALIMA. I unfriended him when you two broke up.

EMILY. Halima, why would you do that? How am I going to / know –?

HALIMA. I'm a mother of two, I can't stalk your ex-boyfriends for you.

EMILY. Singular. Not plural.

HALIMA. Oh, well then.

EMILY. How are the kids?

HALIMA. Baby is good.

EMILY. What's wrong with Layla?

HALIMA. She's sleepwalking. Last night she took out all her toys.

When I asked her about it this morning, she didn't remember a thing.

EMILY. That's pretty common, right?

HALIMA. I'm afraid it's genetic. So I started doing research.

EMILY. Do you or Nigel sleepwalk?

HALIMA. I never told you about my sister?

EMILY. You have a sister?

HALIMA. My identical twin. She used to sleepwalk all the time.

When she was four, she sleepwalked off a balcony in Cairo.

EMILY. Oh my god. Did she?

HALIMA. She died.

EMILY. I am so –

HALIMA. And once while sound asleep, I walked to my car, started the engine and drove off. I woke up on the side of the road. I was dreaming about my sister. She was pressing down on my eyelids with her tiny thumbs. In my dream, she was still a little girl, even though if she survived, she'd be a woman. She would look exactly like me.

EMILY. Oh God. That must –

HALIMA. Now my daughter's four years old.

Do you think my sister is trying to take her away from me?

EMILY. ...No?

Jesus Christ Halima.

I think she should see a sleep specialist.

And maybe you might consider seeing a therapist –

HALIMA. Therapy is a sign of weakness.

EMILY. That's not true. I think it would be good to talk to someone.

I mean, you're my best friend *(Baby begins to cry.)* and you've never even mentioned your twin.

HALIMA. My children are my therapy. Don't worry about me.

EMILY. Yeah but.

This is all really terrible. What are you going to do about it?

HALIMA. Do about it? *(Baby cries louder.)* Hold on.

(**HALIMA** *begins to coo and sing to her baby.*)

EMILY. Can you sleep in the same bed as Layla?

HALIMA. *(In between coos.)* Nigel won't allow it. He thinks I'm mollycoddling her. British men.

(Crying and cooing.)

I gotta feed Baby. Send me a link though, I'll try to listen to your radio thing.

EMILY. I'm not sure if they record the show. Can't you listen while your feeding?

(Sharp wail of Baby.)

HALIMA. I gotta-I gotta-I gotta.

EMILY. No, don't worry about it. It's not *important...*

(*Sound of fumbling hanging up.*)

Five

(Telephone rings.)

EMILY. Hello?

DJ LOKI. Whatupwhatupwhatup. This is DJ Loki from Z 101.3 Hot Spot.

Do I have... Emily on the line?

EMILY. Yes?

DJ LOKI. You got the scenario? We need you to be sexy, alluring, really-hot-sounding, looking for a hook up. Iris just heard us award Office Stud of the week to Keoni.

Just based on his voice on the air, you think he's aaaaaaawesome. You are calling because you've decided, what the heck, I should call and see if theres a chance. It's a shot in the dark but if you don't call now, you'll <u>die</u> without knowing if he was your looooooovvee connection.

DJ SOLANGE. Heeeeey. DJ Solange here. You got that Emily? Or should I say, Iris? Just remember, you're a confident woman, killer bod, killer personality, and you are looking for an awwweeeeeeesome guy and is Keoooooooni interested? Got it?

*(**EMILY** clears her throat repeatedly.)*

Still on the line?

EMILY. I'm here.

DJ SOLANGE. Okay. Here we go.

DJ LOKI. You're going to hear two clicks then we're live.

(Two faint sounds of something.)

EMILY. *(Dead air.)* ... Heeyyy. *(Throat clearing.)*

Hi I'm Iris –

DJ SOLANGE.   – Don't say your name first. Nobody does that.

EMILY. We're not on the air? –

(*Z 101.3 intro blares.*)

DJ LOKI. This is Z 101.3, Hot Spot with DJ Loki –

DJ SOLANGE. And DJ Solange on your FM morning drive.

You just heard from Keoni, the Office Stud of the Week.

(*Office Stud of the Week sound cue.*)

DJ LOKI. Smoking!

DJ SOLANGE. Would you do him?

DJ LOKI. Sweetheart, Loki don't swing that way. But if I was a chick, FOGETTABOUT it.

DJ SOLANGE. How about you, Grandpa Z?

> (**GRANDPA Z** *is played by* **DJ LOKI**, *with a ridiculous old person voice.*)

GRANDPA Z. He sounds like a Sex Machine. SMACK DAT MONKEY!!!!!!!!!

(*Smack Dat Monkey sound cue.*)

DJ SOLANGE. Hold on, Grandpa Z, I think you have some competition.

EMILY. ...Hey. I was just calling to see if Keoni was um. Single?

DJ SOLANGE. Oh sister, we haven't even asked him yet. But didn't he sound hot or what?

GRANDPA Z. Smoking hot!

DJ SOLANGE. Hold up Grandpa Z, DJ Solange might want to keep Keoni for herself.

DJ LOKI. Allll right!!!

DJ SOLANGE. Tell us about yourself. We're going to see if we can make a Z 101.3 Looooove connection.

(Musical underscore begins.)*

EMILY. I'm... I'm a desirable woman and a fitness enthusiast!!! I've never done this before, but after hearing Keoni's voice on your show, I just got a feeling about him.

So I thought, what the heck, I'd call to see if I have a chance.

I'm twenty nine – twenty four-years-old, green eyes, extremely lithe.

(Record scratch, music out.)

DJ LOKI. Oh ho ho. Lithe? You sound aaaaaaaweeeesome.

GRANDPA Z. SUUUUUUUUPPPERAAAAWWWWEE EESOME.

DJ SOLANGE. Calm down boys, she's calling about Keoni, remember?

DJ LOKI. Ohhhhhh yeeeeeahhh.

(Restart underscore.)

EMILY. Basically I can get anyone I want, being a beautiful, desirable woman, but there's an emptiness inside of me. An emptiness that I don't know how to fill. I feel like a mollusk clinging to a rock, not moving, waiting for an octopus to pry me open.

(A brief moment of dead air.)

---

* A license to produce TODAY IS MY BIRTHDAY does not include a performance license for any third-party or copyrighted music. Licensees should create an original composition or use music in the public domain. For further information, please see the Music and Third-Party Materials Use Note on page iii.

DJ LOKI. Alllll riggghtttt. Sounds like we got a girl who knows how to paaaartee.

GRANDPA Z. She should go out with GRANDPA Z. Want me to take you out Grandpa style?

(Horny **GRANDPA Z** *sound cue.)*

EMILY. No?

DJ SOLANGE. Hoooaaahhhh!!!!! She showed you, Grandpa Z. What's your name, honey?

EMILY. My name is um. Iris.

DJ SOLANGE. So Um Iris. What would you say if Z 101.3 Hot Spot –

DJ LOKI. With DJ Loki –

DJ SOLANGE. – AND DJ So-lange, could get Keeeeeooooonnni on the tele-phon-eee?

EMILY. Oh! Really?

That would be – uh...

(Dead air.)

DJ LOKI. That would be aaaawwwwessssooome. Wouldn't it, Iris?

EMILY. Oh yeah!

DJ SOLANGE. Hahaha. Isn't she grreeeeaat? Now, let's see if we can connect these two love birds.

If you think Iris and Keoni have a looooooooveee connection, hit us up on Twitter or Facebook!

(Dialing. Telephone rings.)

KEONI. Sup.

GRANDPA Z. HAH! Listen to this guy. Sup. So manly.

DJ LOKI. Okay, Keoni, our Office Stud of the WEEK.

(Office Stud of the Week Sound Cue.)

I got my home-girl Iris on the line. Twenty four-years-old. *Lithe,* that means she keeps it tight, yo, and she has sum'thing she'd like to ask YOU.

KEONI. Sure.

EMILY. Hey. Keoni. Do you want to go out sometime?

KEONI. Sure.

(Deafening sound of bells, whistles hoots.)

DJ LOKI. DA BRADDAH said YES. Z 101.3, keeping da spot HOT for yoooooouuuuuu.

(Cue intro to a contemporary Jawaiian song, a song in the style of Natural Vibrations' "Maybe". Music fades.)*

EMILY. Hello?

DJ Loki?

DJ Solange?

Keoni?

Grandpa Z?

---

* A license to produce TODAY IS MY BIRTHDAY does not include a performance license for "MAYBE." The publisher and author suggest that the licensee contact ASCAP or BMI to ascertain the music publisher and contact such music publisher to license or acquire permission for performance of the song. If a license or permission is unattainable for "MAYBE," the licensee may not use the song in TODAY IS MY BIRTHDAY but should create an original composition in a similar style or use a similar song in the public domain. For further information, please see the Music and Third-Party Materials Use Note on page iii.

Six

(Telephone rings.)

EMILY. CDF Solutions, this is Emily.

RICHARD. Emily. Richard. Quick question for ya about Bullet 26C, in Section 17 Chapter 5 of the Robertson Geo Displacement Drilling Fluid Plan.

EMILY. Should I come by your office?

RICHARD. No can do, about to go in a meeting. You got it in front of you?

(Sound of massive paper shuffling.)

EMILY. Err.

RICHARD. I can wait. *(Microsecond later.)* Do you have it?

EMILY. Section... Bullet 26... C? Yep.

RICHARD. You've rewritten some of the language on Displacement Boring. Quote: "Upon reaching the desired depth, a plugged hollow-stem, continuous-flight auger is drilled into the ground. The rate of auger penetration during the pile installation has an impact on the pile performance. During auger penetration, the rate of penetration should be such that there is minimal release of lateral stress due to soil removal. During auger penetration there is always some lateral displacement," end quote.

EMILY. Was that not...

RICHARD. The original section was three times this length.

EMILY. I thought it was unnecessarily circuitous. I combined the sections about auger penetration, and moved that section about the um... lateral feed of soil with the auger... um...

RICHARD. The auger tip!

EMILY. ...into Section 28B. Doesn't it read better?

RICHARD. You need to stop taking creative liberties.

EMILY. Richard. This is a construction overview plan for a build site.

Shouldn't it be clear and direct?

RICHARD. Sometimes these things are in for a reason. For legal reasons.

I know you're a "professional" writer and that this is really boring –

EMILY. NO. This is fascinating, important work and I am so...

Being a professional writer means I need to be adaptive. I just had a misguided...

RICHARD. Notion?

EMILY. A misguided notion about what you wanted. Richard. I'm so sorry about this.

RICHARD. You keep at it.

EMILY. So I know Trisha is coming back soon, and I was wondering if we could schedule a meeting about –

RICHARD. There's my one p.m. See you. Great work, Emily.

Oh hey. Keiko told me you were late because you were on the radio?

Super cool.

(Click.)

Seven

(Telephone rings.)

EMILY. This is Emily. You know what to do.

(Beep.)

MOM. Hey sweetie, so Auntie Feng Feng and I tried to listen to your radio article.

But it was just this Mexican radio station. I listened all morning.

So if you were on, I couldn't understand what you were saying.

It was 100.3, wasn't it? Did you call your father?

Love you.

This is your mother.

(Click.)

Eight

(Telephone rings.)

HALIMA. Mom?

EMILY. Hey Halima. It's Emily.

HALIMA. Fantastic, I thought you were my mother-in-law. Hey, I never got your link.

EMILY. They don't archive the show.

HALIMA. Oh dang.

EMILY. But I'll be on again next Tuesday for the aftermath of "The Date with Keoni."

HALIMA. Wow. You're really making a thing out of – DO NOT PUT THAT UP YOUR NOSE.

I don't care. I don't care. NO. No. NO. Because Mommy said so.

EMILY. Is everything going okay with Layla? And the sleepwalking?

HALIMA. I don't know yet.

EMILY. I know I've been caught up with myself over the last couple months... with the breakup and the move, and... but if you want to talk about that or your dead twin.

I really miss you.

HALIMA. I miss you too. So anyway, I think Nige's been reading my diary.

EMILY. That's. Ew. How do you know?

HALIMA. He had a funny look on his face when I came in the other night. And then he made me watch *Nell*, and then asked me if it reminded me of anything.

EMILY. *Nell?*

HALIMA. I wrote about my sister after talking to you. And Nell's sister died too.

They had that twin language – *tay ina*

EMILY & HALIMA. *tay ina win*

Chicka, chicka, chickabee.

EMILY. Holy shit.

I had forgotten about that.

HALIMA. I think maybe he's been reading it for a long time.

EMILY. So... how do you feel about that?

(Thud. Sharp wailing of Layla.)

HALIMA. Oh that fuck – dging coffee table. Sweetie you're okay. You're okay.

(Crying and cooing.)

Honey, I gotta-gotta-gotta – I'll try to catch part two?

EMILY. It's okay. It's not. *(Click.) Important.*

Nine

(Telephone rings.)

DAD. Chang residence, you've got Abraham.

EMILY. Mom got you to answer the phone like that too?

DAD. Mimi?

EMILY. Mom wanted me to call you?

DAD. She didn't tell you?

EMILY. No, are you okay? Are you sick?

DAD. No. no. Goodness.

EMILY. You scared me.

DAD. No, I'm fine.

Your mother and I are getting divorced.

EMILY. What?

Divorced?

DAD. Well.

EMILY. Dad. Seriously? Where is this coming from?

You've been married for forty-one years.

DAD. Were both sixty three. It's our last shot of being with other people.

EMILY. Do you want to be with other people?

DAD. That's not what I meant.

EMILY. I can't even... not even a trial separation?

Dad, this is terrible.

DAD. Well, I don't know sweetie. We gave it a good run. And you're all grown up.

We didn't think it would affect you that much.

EMILY. I moved back home.

DAD. But not to be with us, right? Your mother always complains that we never see you.

Anyhoo, you want us to be happy, don't you?

EMILY. Will you be happy if you get a divorce?

DAD. ...I'll have more time to work on projects.

EMILY. Projects?

DAD. I was listening to a program on NPR, and a composer noticed that the hum of his copier, telephone, and radiator each had a tone. And together they formed a chord that he'd hear continuously throughout the day that affected his mood. A major chord is happy, a minor cord is sad. So, I've been feeling a little sad lately –

EMILY. Because you're getting a divorce?

DAD. So I got out my little pitch pipe. *(Plays a sound from a pitch pipe.)*

EMILY. Dad!

DAD. And the wind from the window, my computer, and my printer make a C, E-flat, and G-flat chord. It's a diminished triad, the outer fifth of which is a tri-tone, i.e. Satan's music. So when I get my new apartment, I'm going to shop around for appliances that harmonize.

EMILY. You're moving out?

DAD. Your mother has more stuff.

EMILY. Was this your decision or Mom's?

DAD. You know your mother.

EMILY. So she's the one that wants the divorce?

DAD. That's not what I said.

EMILY. Isn't it?

DAD. Mm.

EMILY. Then why did she make me call you?

DAD. Beats me, hon.

EMILY. I have to go.

　　　(Click.)

Ten

(Telephone rings.)

MOM. *(Sweet as pie.)* Aloha, you've reached the voicemail of Grace Chang. I'm so sorry I'm not here to pick up the phone right now, but please leave a detailed message and I'll get right back to you as soon as possible. A hui ho! Have yourself a beautiful day now!

(Beep.)

EMILY. Moooooom. What are you doing to dad? God damn it Mom. Why didn't you tell me? This is so fucked up. Are you fucking other men? What the hell?

AAAARUGHHHHHH. FUUUUUUCCCCCKKKKK KKK YOOOOUUUU.

(Beep.)

GENERIC FEMALE VOICE. If you're satisfied with your message, press 1. To erase your message, press.

(Beep.)

GENERIC FEMALE VOICE.	**EMILY**.
Message sent. To mark this message as urgent press	WHAT! I hit erase. Oh God.
	Oh god. Oh *(Pressing buttons.)* my god
Invalid option. To mark this message with regular –	Fuckkkk. Fuck. Fuck. Fuck. Fuck. Fuck. Fuck.

(Sound of **EMILY** *pressing buttons.)*

GENERIC FEMALE VOICE. Thank you.

(A moment.)

EMILY. Fuck.

(Click.)

Eleven

(Saccharine Hawaiian instrumental music underscores the commercial.*)

DJ SOLANGE. Honolulu Repertory Theater is now selling tickets to their annual Kala Gala following their acclaimed production of Edward Sakamoto's *The Taste of Kona Coffee.* Visit Honolulu Repertory Theater dot org to bring quality local theater to your community.

(Music out. Z 101.3 Hot Spot Intro blares.)

DJ LOKI. Z 101.3 Hotspot back at ya and we're back with the Office Stud of Last Week, Keoooooni *(Office Stud of the Week Sound Cue.)* to hear about his date with the lovely IRIS. So you two lovebirds, how'd it go?

EMILY. ...Good.

GRANDPA Z. She look good enough for Grandpa Z?

KEONI. She's stunning. Great smile. Beautiful eyes –

EMILY. – I'm a yoga instructor!

DJ SOLANGE. And how about him?

EMILY. He's 6'2. Sandy hair. Green-gray eyes. Held all the doors for me.

DJ LOKI. Where'd you go on this date?

KEONI. I took her to a restaurant.

EMILY. On a pier!

GRANDPA Z. Oh ho ho. Sounds expensive.

---

* A license to produce TODAY IS MY BIRTHDAY does not include a performance license for any third-party or copyrighted music. Licensees should create an original composition or use music in the public domain. For further information, please see the Music and Third-Party Materials Use Note on page iii.

(Ca-Ching sound cue.)

KEONI. She's worth it.

DJ SOLANGE. Aww. How sweet.

KEONI. Then we went dancing. She's a great dancer.

EMILY. We danced the merengue!!!

(An upbeat song in the style of "Rhythm of the Night" blasts.*)

GRANDPA Z. Did you show her your moves on and off the dance floor?

*(Horny **GRANDPA** sound cue.)*

KEONI. A gentleman never tells.

DJ SOLANGE. So sweet. Are you going to ask Miss Iris out on date number two?

KEONI. Iris? What do you say?

EMILY. I'd love to!!!

(Resounding bells, whistles, foghorn. Arooogah.)

DJ SOLANGE. There you have it. Post suggestions on Facebook or Twitter for where Keoni should take Iris on their SECOND date. And Happy Birthday to Jayden J. Here's a song for you from your honey-girl Charlene brought to you by Z 101.3 Hotspot.

(An upbeat song in the style of "Island Style" plays.*)

---

* A license to produce TODAY IS MY BIRTHDAY does not include a performance license for any third-party or copyrighted music. Licensees should create an original composition or use music in the public domain. For further information, please see the Music and Third-Party Materials Use Note on page iii.

Twelve

(Telephone rings.)

SEBASTIAN-VOICE RECORDING.

Hey this is Sebastian. You   *(Beep.)*
know what to do.

> *(**EMILY** has been watching Nell's "tay ina wind" scene. **EMILY** has one too many glasses of wine.)*

EMILY. Hey Sebastian. It's Emily. I was just calling to see how you are. I've started acting. On the radio? It feels kind of natural for me, actually. Because most of the time, I can't stand myself at all. Like, not the sound of my voice or my thoughts, or the cadence of my steps. I don't mean that in a self-deprecating way. I just.

GENERIC FEMALE VOICE.

If you're satisfied with   *(Beep.)*
your message, press 1.

Message erased. If you   *(Beep.)*
would like to record a
new –

EMILY. – When you broke up with me via text message, I was crossing Houston Street and got hit by a car. Not like, terribly so, but you know, it happened. So I ran into the subway before the driver could get out. And I started crying. Just really hard.

Not from you breaking up with me but from the shock of being hit by a car.

Sitting across from me was an old, steely-looking man. I want to say he was a priest but he probably wasn't, since it was two in the morning. Just before he got off the train, he took me by the shoulders, looked into my eyes and said,

"Don't cry on the subway. You hear? Don't cry on the subway."

I think he's my guardian angel.

GENERIC FEMALE VOICE.

If you're satisfied with   *(Beep.)*
your message, press 1.

Message erased. If you   *(Beep.)*
would like –

EMILY. I just wanted you to know, I've met a wonderful man. His name is Keoni.

So you can stop worrying about me, because I don't worry about you.

But if something's wrong, you can always let me know. I'm here for you.

    (Beep.)

GENERIC FEMALE VOICE. Message sent.

Thirteen

(Telephone rings.)

KURT. Yellow.

EMILY. Hey Kurt. It's Emily.

KURT. Hey, how did the radio thing turn out?

EMILY. Pretty good, I think.

KURT. Thanks so much for doing it. Free airtime, you know.

We're trying to get people – Danielle, I asked for oat milk – to buy tickets to our gala.

EMILY. Right, I don't care. I was just wondering if you knew the other actor?

His pseudonym was Keoni.

KURT. It's Kai. Right?

EMILY. I'm asking you.

KURT. Kai. Pretty sure.

EMILY. Do you have his phone number?

KURT. Why do you need it?

EMILY. Are you seriously giving me a hard time about this?

(Text sound.)

KURT. Just texted it to you.

EMILY. Thanks.

KURT. Sure thing. Wanna come to the Kala Gala?

EMILY. I guess.

KURT. You want one ticket or two?

EMILY. One. No. Two. <u>Two</u>.

(Click.)

Fourteen

(Telephone rings.)

GENERIC FEMALE VOICE. You have reached 8-0-8-3-4-8-1-2-9-9. Please leave a message.

(Beep.)

EMILY. Hi Kai. This – FUCK.

(Beep.)

GENERIC FEMALE VOICE. If you're satisfied with your –

(Beep.)

EMILY. Hey Kai. Emily, here. You might. Uh. You might know me as *Iris*. I was your uh scene partner on the radio a few days ago. Anyhoo. I'm new in town, well, I grew up here but I'm back! And uh... I thought it would be nice to meet other people in the uh *acting* community. So let me know if you want to grab a coffee. Or a drink.

Or some dinner, or something. Hahaha. Okay! Byee. You take care!

(Fumbling. Beep.)

#

(Telephone rings.)

GENERIC FEMALE VOICE. You have reached 8-0-8-3-4-8-1-2-9-. Please leave a message.

(Beep.)

EMILY. Hey...fake Keoni. This is fake Iris. Emily. This is Emily. I called a few days ago. I was just giving you a call to make sure I had the right number. Never know with these generic voice messages...ha ha ha! Also, I wanted to let you know that Kurt gave me your number, that's how I got it. Not from the radio station. He figured it would be a good idea for us to meet, because we're both actors, so I was following up with that. Okay! You take care. Bye! – Oh also, I have tickets to the HRT Gala. So if you want to come with, ha ha ha! That'd be super great! Ha ha ha ha ha! Okay. Byeee!

(Click.)

Fifteen

(Telephone rings.)

*(**EMILY** and **LANDON** at their respective desks.)*

LANDON. New Pacific Design, Landon.

EMILY. Hey, Landon.

LANDON. Yo.

(Text sounds.)

I just texted you two layouts for a children's clothing website.

Which version is cuter? Rabbits or ducks?

EMILY. Rabbits make me think of Easter but ducks are terrifying.

LANDON. Right, you have that weird bird thing.

EMILY. It's the flapping, and the beaks, and the talons.

LANDON. Maybe I should change it to bears. Bears are cute right? I mean, they only maul.

EMILY. And at any moment they could peck out your eyes or –

LANDON. We're switching gears.

Are you writing?

EMILY. You sound like my mother. I tried. No one responded to my queries.

LANDON. Every article you've written is "New York-centric."

Write something local, shop it around. You wen call my maddah?

(Call waiting sound.)

EMILY. Hold on.

(Call waiting sound.)

LANDON. Yep.

(Call waiting sound.)

EMILY. Never mind, it's my mother, sending to voicemail. What was I... Oh right –

I have two tickets to this Gala, it's kind of this fancy dress up thing.

LANDON. You need a date.

EMILY. Ye-ah.

LANDON. You're asking me right? Because I am bone-tired of setting up straight people.

EMILY. Yes. However. There is a guy I'm hoping will be there.

We're both in the theater community and this is a theater gala.

LANDON. Nice.

Wait, since when did you do theater?

EMILY. The radio thing!

LANDON. That's not theater.

EMILY. It's for HRT. Do you remember Kurt? He's the artistic director.

He was a senior when we were sophomores?

LANDON. That D-bag? Didn't you give him a blowie spring break freshman year in his Dad's PT Cruiser?

EMILY. Your memory is extraordinarily...

LANDON. Didn't he marry that psychopathic pediatric surgeon?

EMILY. Snežana's not crazy, she's just... she's really pretty.

LANDON. Better be, with a name like that.

EMILY. She's from Belarus.

LANDON. Bella-rude.

EMILY. Anyway. This guy I'm hoping to.

LANDON. To fuck.

EMILY. Eeeueehhh... I don't really know what he looks like or anything about him except his name and his voice –

LANDON. You want me to make him jealous?

EMILY. I just want to meet him. Jealous/ might be...

LANDON. I'm in!

(Click.)

Sixteen

(Telephone rings.)

EMILY. This is Emily. You know what to do.

(Beep.)

MOM. EMILY ROBERTA LIEN-HUA HAILIʻŌPUA CHANG. Call me back right now.

(Beat.) I assume you've talked to your father.

This is your mother.

(Beep.)

GENERIC FEMALE VOICE. Message erased.

Seventeen

(Telephone rings.)

EMILY. This is Emily. You know what to do.

(Beep.)

LANDON. *(Whispering.)* Hey girl. I'm having a minor but impactful crisis right now.

I'm really-really-really super sorry but I can't come to your gala tonight. Sorry!

But let's hang out soon, okay?

(Beep.)

GENERIC FEMALE VOICE. Message erased.

Eighteen

(Telephone rings.)

DAD. Chang residence. You've got Abraham.

EMILY. Dad. It's Emily.

DAD. Oh hello.

(Offstage.) It's Mimi.

MOM. *Who?*

DAD. Emily.

MOM. *(comes out from behind louver.)* WHO?

DAD. EMILY. OUR DAUGHTER.

MOM. *(Offstage.)* Oh.

EMILY. Is mom there?.

DAD. Did you want to talk to Mimi?

MOM Does she have something to say to me?

DAD. Your mother wants to know if you have anything to say to her.

EMILY. *Nope.* I was calling for you.

DAD. Oh how nice.

MOM. *(Offstage.) There's no stamps.*

DAD. Check the junk drawer.

MOM. *(Offstage.)* I did.

DAD. Well, didn't I put some on the refrigerator? The sushi magnet?

MOM. *(Offstage.) Oh.*

EMILY. The Kala Gala is tonight at the Hanohano Room.

(**EMILY** *peppers "dads" periodically through the next monologue.*)

MOM. *(comes out from behind louver.) Nope.*

DAD. *(Offstage.)* If we were all out, I could've bought more at the post office, I was there two days ago.

MOM. *(through the louver.) So should I time travel?*

DAD. No. That wasn't a criticism –

MOM. *(through the louver.) You're not helping me.*

DAD. Well, I know that doesn't help you – I'm just saying I'm pretty sure there are stamps in the house but I could have also bought more.

MOM. *(offstage) Could've?*

DAD. I know that doesn't help you now, that's not what I'm saying.

MOM. *(offstage) Sounds like it.*

DAD. That's not what I'm saying.

MOM. *(offstage)* You're being argumentative.

DAD. I'm not being argumentative. I'm just saying. That's not what I'm saying.

MOM. *(offstage) What are you saying??*

DAD. If you needed stamps.

MOM. *(offstage)* How is this you anticipating my needs?

DAD. I guess I could have – Did you check inside the turtle?

MOM. *(offstage)* Oh.

EMILY. DAD.

DAD. *(To* **EMILY.***)* Your mother wants to mail you something.

EMILY. Please God. Not another article.

DAD. *(Offstage.)* Is it an article?

EMILY. Don't ask her!

MOM. *(offstage) Yeah.*

DAD. It's an article and a check. She says none of those magazines have hired you, so you need money.

EMILY. CDF Solutions is going to bring me on as a long-term contractor.

DAD. *(Offstage.)* Mimi says don't mail the check! They like her at that place.

> (**MOM** *comes out and rips the check.*)

EMILY. Also, I'm trying to think of a local human-interest story to write on spec. Any ideas?

DAD. Mmm. Well, Bill Tapia is about to turn a hundred-and-four.

EMILY. Who?

DAD. He's the world's oldest performing musician. Ukulele player.

Maybe you could talk to him.

EMILY. Do you know how to reach him?

DAD. *(Wistful.)* I think Patsy does.

MOM. *(through louver, and pushing away curtain) Patsy does what?*

DAD. We're just talking about an idea for a story.

MOM. *(offstage) Huh.*

EMILY. DAD. I was just calling you because Landon cancelled for this gala tonight and I was wondering if you wanted to be my date. You could dust off the old suit.

DAD. I don't think I could fit into any of my old suits.

MOM. *(offstage) You two just go on, talk talk talk.*

DAD. I don't understand what you want me to ask her.

MOM. *(offstage) You're being hostile!*

DAD. I'm not being hostile!

EMILY. ... Some of the members of the Philharmonic will be there. Maybe we can slip them a Hamilton and ask them to play some Mendelssohn.

DAD. Is Roger Takeda still on contrabass clarinet?

EMILY. Maybe he'd be there.

DAD. I don't know if he'd remember me.

EMILY. He invites you to his holiday party every year. There's still time, we can run out and buy you a new aloha shirt? It'll be really great.

DAD. I don't think I can.

EMILY. It'd be good for you to get out of the house.

DAD. Well... if you want to see a movie sometime, that might be nice.

    (Click. **DAD** *hangs up.)*

EMILY. I don't want to go alone.

Nineteen

(Telephone rings.)

EMILY. This is Emily, you know what to do.

(Beep.)

(The haunting music of a string quartet.* It goes on for a while.)

DAD. Hey sweetie. As you might have guessed, that's Mendelssohn String Quartet No 6 in F minor, Op. 80, 3rd Movement with Itzhak Perlman and Bernard Haitink conducting the Concertgebouw Orchestra, 1977 recording.

Your pops is having an adagio night in.

I hope you are having a wonderful evening.

I'm sure you look beautiful.

(Beat.)

This is your father.

(Beep.)

GENERIC FEMALE VOICE. Message saved.

---

* A license to produce TODAY IS MY BIRTHDAY does not include a performance license for any third-party or copyrighted music. Licensees should create an original composition or use music in the public domain. For further information, please see the Music and Third-Party Materials Use Note on page iii.

Twenty

(Door buzzes. An inebriated **EMILY** *answers. Intercom feedback.)*

EMILY. Hell-o?

*(***KURT** *and* **EMILY** *have a conversation through the intercom.)*

KURT. I just wanted to make sure you got in okay.

EMILY. I'm sorry for all the things I said at your fête.

KURT. Gala.

EMILY. Did I win anything?

KURT. You won dinner for two at Doraku at the Silent Auction.

EMILY. Ooooohhhh.

KURT. Maybe you should throw up.

EMILY. Maybe *you* should throw up.

KURT. Jesus Christ Emily.

EMILY. How come Snezzlasagna doesn't like me?

KURT. Snežana likes you fine.

EMILY. I mean she hates all women, mostly equally, but she 'specially hates ME.

KURT. That's unfair.

EMILY. You told her that I had been trying to call Kai?

KURT. I thought it was sweet. Life imitating art, or something.

EMILY. WHAT?

KURT. Do you need help? I wanted to make sure you weren't passed out in your hallway.

Buzz me in.

EMILY. I can't let you see me like this.

KURT. I just saw you like –

EMILY. Snezz-your wife said Kai thought the voicemails were weird. And that he didn't even do the radio show. Kai's friend did the last few gigs. She used the word gig.

Was this a paid opportunity? KURT.

KURT. Nuuh – you waved your fee in exchange for free advertising for HRT.

Did you ask for his friends name?

EMILY. I was too embarrassed. I came across like a stalker!

KURT. How many times did you call him?

EMILY. That's not the point.

KURT. I'm going. Snežana's waiting in the car. Drink a glass of water.

EMILY. You drink a glass of water.

KURT. Bye Emily.

EMILY. KURT. Are you there???? KUUUUUUUUUU UUUUUUURRRRRTTTT.

KURT. *(Slightly out of breath.)* What's wrong?

EMILY. I wanna go back on the radio.

KURT. You do?

EMILY. Why do you sound so surprised?

KURT. The Z 101.3 people said you sounded a little hesitant.

EMILY. I was acting like a shy woman about to asked the guy out. Hello!

KURT. I thought the scenario called for confident and sexy.

EMILY. I embody those qualities!!! *(To herself.)* I embody those qualities...

KURT. Do you really want to do this?

EMILY. I WANNA BE A STAR.

Did you even hear me on the radio? It aired two weeks in a row.

KURT. Missed it. Sorreee.

EMILY. I was luminous.

KURT. I'm going, okay?

EMILY. I'm going to be super embarrassed about this in like. Ten hours.

KURT. Take care Emily. If you still want to do the radio thing, text me in the morning. I guess.

(Intercom feedback.)

Twenty One

(Telephone rings.)

EMILY. This is Emily. You know what to do.

HALIMA. Hey girl.

So Nige's definitely been reading my diary.

To test things out I wrote, "Sex with my husband has become a task."

Then today I found a smudge.

A red, sticky smudge from his jam hands right below the word "task."

The bastard was reading my personal private thoughts over jam and toast while I was taking Layla to preschool.

I'm thinking about writing some false entries, just to mess with him.

What do you think?

Love you.

Twenty Two

(Z 101.3 intro blares.)

DJ LOKI. Oh Yeah! This is Z 101.3 hotspot with DJ Loooooookiiiiii

DJ SOLANGE. And DJ Soooolaaaaaange. Today we are back on our Hump Day Wednesday with our loooove expert, Dr. Johannes Connection, for the Love Connection.

> *(**DJ LOKI** speaks with a Ludwig Von Drake-the Disney Duck with a German Accent.)*

> *(Dr. Johannes Connection Intro.)*

DR. JOHANNES CONNECTION. Guten Tag. So glad to be back, my esteemed colleagues.

GRANDPA Z. Yeah, yeah Dr. Fancy Pants!

DJ LOKI. Our first caller is Kahikina, a young woman from Kaaawa *(Ka-a-a-va.)* who's having a pretty tricky time with her hubby.

> *(Melodramatic instrumentals underscore **EMILY**'s speech. **EMILY** speaks like she is reading from a script, but she gains momentum.)*

EMILY. We've been married for five years, and it's been total bliss.

But ever since I gave birth to the twins, he's been coming home later and later.

Finally, I followed him one night and discovered he's been driving to my mother's house. Through the window, I saw them kissing passionately.

Dr. Connection, what should I do?

Could my _husband_ be having an affair with my _mother_?????????

(Record scratch.)

DR. JOHANNES CONNECTION. This is very distressing, very distressing indeed.

Your husband probably does love you but is feeling his sexual needs unmet.

He still imagines a future with you, which is why he is turning to your mother.

EMILY. But what did I do to drive him into her arms?!?

DJ LOKI. Dr. Connection, how can Z 101.3 Hotspot with DJ Loki

DJ SOLANGE. And DJ Solange

DJ LOKI. Help this poor woman?

DR. JOHANNES CONNECTION. We must call your husband.

ALL. GASP.

EMILY. No! I can't face him.

GRANDPA Z. DO IT!!!!

DJ LOKI. And for our Z 101.3 listeners out there, Tweet or Facebook suggestions if you think Kahikina from Kaaawa should give her husband a second chance or

(Hasta la vista sound cue.)

DJ LOKI & SOLANGE. KICK HIM TO THE CURB!

(Kicking husband to the curb sound cue part 1 & part 2.)

GRANDPA Z. Yea! Dump the Chump! Want me take you out grandpa style?

(Horny Grandpa sound cue.)

DJ LOKI. Okaaaaay here goes nothing, right Kahikina?

EMILY. Um. Right!

(Telephone rings.)

KEONI. Hello?

DJ SOLANGE. Is this Sergio *(Beep.)*

KEONI. Yes?

DJ SOLANGE. This is DJ Soooolaaaaange from Z 101.3 Hotspot, and you're on the air.

KEONI. Can I help you?

(CukooCukoo.)

DR. JOHANNES CONNECTION. This is Dr. Johannes Connection, MD, und I'm here with your wife, Kahikina

EMILY. Hi Sergio.

KEONI. Kini?!?!? Oh my God. What are you doing on this show??!!??!!??

DJ SOLANGE. She has a question she'd like to ask you.

EMILY. *(Sotto voice.)* Do you remember me?

KEONI. ...um. You're my wife?

DJ SOLANGE. And she's calling to ask you.

EMILY. Right. Uh. Why do you drive to my mother's house after work?

KEONI. This is going to hurt... I'm in love with your mother. I didn't know how to tell you!?!

EMILY. How could you do this to me... ??!?!?!?!?!?!?!?

KEONI. This is terrible. I'm sick. I love you both so much. I can't decide.

DJ SOLANGE. You must <u>choose</u>. What do you think, Doc?

DR. JOHANNES CONNECTION. I recommend you spend time apart, clear your heads. Jonathan, I think –

EMILY. We should get dinner.

DR. JOHANNES CONNECTION, KEONI & SOLANGE. What?

EMILY. Face to face. In real life.

GRANDPA Z. IS this real life?

EMILY. Shut up Grandpa Z. Eight p.m. This Friday. Doraku. Okay?

DJ SOLANGE. Girl, he's hooking up with your mama.

EMILY. What do you say?

KEONI. Uh, yeah. Okay. Cool.

(Click. Z101.3 Outtro.)

Twenty Two: B

(Telephone rings.)

MAKANA. Oh.

EMILY. Hey Makana? I got your email. You want me to move out this weekend?

MAKANA. Can we talk about this when I get home? I'm at work right now.

EMILY. Then why didn't you bring it up then so we can discuss it?

MAKANA. I was trying to give you time to *process.*

EMILY. I know you love your boyfriend.

MAKANA. I really love Zinn. He's incredible. He's getting kicked out of his loft space.

Plus you're always drinking my milk and then you were shouting on the intercom?

And you and I aren't friend-friends, were just roommates – no offense.

EMILY. My financial situation is really up in the air right now.

MAKANA. But you're working at that fancy engineering office downtown.

EMILY. For a little while longer and then I'm not sure.

MAKANA. Whoopsy.

EMILY. This is really the worst time to move. The University is in session so there's no cheap housing. And I can't ask my parents, because –

MAKANA. Stay with your parents for free! Hey! That's even better. I gotta go back to work.

Don't hate me!

Twenty Three

(Telephone rings. Sounds of a construction site.)

RICHARD. Richard.

EMILY. Hey! Richard! This is Emily.

RICHARD. Who?

EMILY. Emily? I'm the assistant technical writer for um. You?

RICHARD. Oh right. Sorry. It's noisy over here.

EMILY. You're not in the office?

RICHARD. I got the calls transferred to my cell.

EMILY. Well, it's my last day, um. Officially. I was hoping we could sit down and talk about –

RICHARD. No can do. I'm on site. It is cra-zee over here. I'm back Monday.

EMILY. I could come in on Monday.

RICHARD. I wouldn't want to make you do that. Look, if you really want to meet, we'll be done here around seven thirty. I'll text you a restaurant near the site at eight. I'll be starving, but yeah, we can talk then.

EMILY. Thanks Richard. I really appreciate this. Oh wait. I kind of have plans at eight ...

RICHARD. That's my window.

EMILY. Uh. Yeah. Okay. I'll see you at eight.

(Click.)

Twenty Four

(Telephone rings. Restaurant ambience.)

HOSTESS. Thank you for calling Doraku, how may I help you this evening?

EMILY. Hi. I have a reservation tonight under the name Emily Chang. I can't make it.

HOSTESS. I can go ahead and cancel that for you.

EMILY. There's someone I'm supposed to meet there.

I don't have his name or his phone number or anything. He's an actor.

(A pause.)

HOSTESS. ... What would you like me to do?

EMILY. I guess if a man comes and asks for a reservation under the name Iris or Emily or uh Kahikina? Can you tell him –

HOSTESS. May I put you on hold? –

(A jazzy instrumental version of a Hawaiian song plays in the style of "Hawaiian Sup'pah Man".* EMILY sighs. Click.)

---

* A license to produce TODAY IS MY BIRTHDAY does not include a performance license for any third-party or copyrighted music. Licensees should create an original composition or use music in the public domain. For further information, please see the Music and Third-Party Materials Use Note on page iii.

Twenty Five

(Telephone rings.)

HALIMA. Hi you've reached Halima. *(Sound of children laughing.)*

Please leave a message and I'll call you back when I can!

(Beep.)

EMILY. Halima, that's really shitty of Nigel but I think you need to –

(Call waiting sound.)

Shit-Oh My God-Sebastian is calling me-What do I do? Okay.

I'm answering.

(A deep breath. She pick ups call waiting.)

Heya...

(Sounds of bar music,* loud and distorted chatter.)

Sebastian? Sebastian, is that you? I can't hear you.

DID YOU BUTT DIAL ME?

SEBASTIAN. *(Indistinct talking and laughter.)*

WOMAN. *(Indistinct talking and a lot of laugher.)*

EMILY. Are you on a date? You son of a –

WOMAN. *(Laughter.)*

---

* A license to produce TODAY IS MY BIRTHDAY does not include a performance license for any third-party or copyrighted music. Licensees should create an original composition or use music in the public domain. For further information, please see the Music and Third-Party Materials Use Note on page iii.

(**EMILY** *listens in on the conversation. The muffled conversation continues back and forth for longer than it should, before she hangs up. Click.*)

Twenty Six

(Telephone rings.)

EMILY. CDF Solutions. This is Emily.

RICHARD. Hi. Emily? Richard... Keiko just emailed me that she saw you come in?

EMILY. Monday bright and early. Did you need to see me in your office?

RICHARD. I'm back on site. Are you sharing a desk with Trisha?

EMILY. Not yet. When she gets here, maybe we should debrief, and figure out where to set up my new office.

RICHARD. Here's the thing...

EMILY. Are you kidding me?

RICHARD. Look, I'll tell it to you straight. There isn't money in the budget for three technical writers. It's been a learning curve, but you've done some great work here, and I can write you a positive letter of recommendation.

EMILY. I thought you said I had a great future ahead of me.

RICHARD. You do. Not in technical writing but...in the kind of writing you like to do...

EMILY. Journalism! I have a Masters Degree from Columbia. I cannot believe you are doing this to me.

RICHARD. I can't believe you're doing this to me. You're making me feel like a real scumbag.

EMILY. Me??? You were interested in my feedback on revamping the High Water Requirements in the Reverse Circulation Rotary Drilling Section!

I asked if I could come in to show you on Monday, you said yes.

RICHARD. I don't recall saying that.

EMILY. That's what you said.

RICHARD. I was dehydrated and exhausted and drunk.

EMILY. Are you pretending you don't remember what happened?

RICHARD. I remember you putting your hand on my arm. I remember you asking for the second round of drinks. You asking where we were going next.

EMILY. Oh my God oh my God. You totally used me.

RICHARD. I am not a predator! *(Whispering.)* I am sorry if I gave you false hope about your position here. But why would I get involved with a co-worker???

I thought we were getting together because your time at CDF Solutions ended and we have a great connection. I had a really nice time. Didn't you?

EMILY. Fuck. Fuck. Fuck.

RICHARD. Wait.

Did you...did you go out with me because you thought you could keep your job?

EMILY. ...

RICHARD. *(With an odd compassion.)* That's really sad, Emily.

EMILY. Yeah well. Great talk. I'm glad you can keep the moral high ground here, Boss.

I'll be heading out now. Do I need to fill anything out?

RICHARD. Check in with Keiko.

Emily, can we –

    (Click.)

Twenty Seven

(Telephone rings.)

DAD. Sinclair Library, Special Music Collections, Dr. Chang speaking.

EMILY. *(Tearful but sort-of-covering it up.)* Hi dad...

DAD. Mimi? Are you okay sweetie?

EMILY. I dont know.

DAD. What do you mean?

EMILY. Nothing. I'm fine. I'm stuck in traffic.

DAD. Why are you driving in the middle of the afternoon. Aren't you at work?

EMILY. What are you listening to?

DAD. Can you hear it?

EMILY. No. But you're always listening to something.

DAD. Charles Ives. One of the fathers of American Modernist Composition.

EMILY. Cool.

*(**EMILY** sniffs.)*

DAD. Are you getting sick?

EMILY. No...

DAD. You shouldn't talk on the phone while driving.

Your mother said Auntie Feng Feng got a ticket just last –

EMILY. You're on speaker. What's his music like? Would I like it?

DAD. Ives was really into mistakes.

EMILY. Maybe I would like him.

DAD. He'd listen to ragtime bands, and the musicians would be drunk and play the wrong notes, and he would notate it. He was inspired by Fourth of July parades, where you could hear several marching bands playing different songs simultaneously.

He would notate the jumble of songs all together and that would be his composition.

It's counterpoint, in a sense. I'll turn it up. Can you hear it?

> *(The opening dissonance of Charles Ives "Central Park in the Dark".*)*

This is *Central Park in the Dark*. Ives evokes the sensation of being in the center of the city at night. It's comprised out of fragments of a ragtime song mixed with a Church hymn and then a marching band number. He put them all together and made something new out of it. And then, you know that song from the frog in Looney Tunes? "Hello my baby, hello my honey?"

EMILY. Yeah.

DAD. That's in there too.

EMILY. Doesn't it sound terrible?

DAD. Some people think so.

It can be beautiful and emotional,

but also cacophonous.

He called it The Grind.

---

* A license to produce TODAY IS MY BIRTHDAY does not include a performance license for any third-party or copyrighted music. Licensees should create an original composition or use music in the public domain. For further information, please see the Music and Third-Party Materials Use Note on page iii.

And it keeps on going,

growing more

and more complex

until it becomes

unintelligible.

(They listen to Charles Ives. Music fades up.)

Twenty Eight

(Telephone rings.)

EMILY. This is Emily. You know what to do.

(Beep.)

HALIMA. The kids are asleep! Why aren't you picking up?

I wrote a false entry in my diary.

Something cruel. Something that would cut.

Then I couldn't stop. Entry after entry of lurid, preposterous infidelities.

Layla was conceived by a San Francisco beatnik bum.

Baby was conceived in the bathroom of a dive bar on St. Mark's.

The thing is, deep down, if he loved me, if he truly knew me,

He'd know they're absurd lies.

But instead he shouts, he weeps that I am unfaithful.

The children are bastards. And he's a cuckold.

"That is ridiculous, you are the only man I have been with for the last ten years. What could I have done that would make you think such a terrible thing?"

And my husband, the father of my children, looks at me with so much love and pain behind his eyes, that I almost forget that

I DESPISE HIM.

He has raped my thoughts and invaded the most personal aspect of me.

Also, Sebastian? What the hell?

Next time that dipshit calls, Do Not Pick Up.

Don't give away your power, girl. You know better.

(Click.)

Twenty Nine

(Telephone rings.)

HOSTESS. Doraku, how may I help you?

EMILY. Hi. This is a long shot, but I cancelled a reservation a few –

HOSTESS. Emily Chang?

EMILY. ...yes?

HOSTESS. Franklin left his number for you. He wanted yours but I couldn't give it out.

EMILY. Franklin?

What does he look like?

HOSTESS. Brown hair, brown eyes, medium build.

EMILY. Is he cute? On scale of 1-10 –

HOSTESS. I will not do that labor for you. You want his number or not? Because I have tables to seat.

EMILY. Yes ma'am.

(Click.)

Thirty

(Telephone rings.)

FRANKLIN. Hello?

EMILY. Hi. This is Emily. We were supposed to meet at –

FRANKLIN. Well hello there.

EMILY. I'm sorry about that. I had a work thing and no way to contact you.

FRANKLIN. I've never been stood up before.

It was a pretty anti-climactic finish to that on-air pick up.

EMILY. It wasn't a pick up.

FRANKLIN. No? Not even for the Z 101.3 Office Stud of the Week?

EMILY. Well, the last time you were *(German accent.)* my husband having und affair with my mother.

FRANKLIN. How do they come up with this stuff?

EMILY. I have no idea. So. I don't know anything about you. Tell me something.

FRANKLIN. Something. Haha. No. What do you want to know?

EMILY. What do you do?

FRANKLIN. I'm a landscape architect. My buddy Kai had a bad case of strep throat and as a joke, I took over this gig for him.

EMILY. So you're not an actor?

FRANKLIN. Nope – Did you just exhale a sigh of relief?

EMILY. It's just that I'm really interested in landscape architecture.

FRANKLIN. Right. I take it you're not an actor either.

EMILY. Actors are the worst. I'm a journalist. I just moved back here from New York City.

FRANKLIN. Where do you work?

EMILY. I. Well, uh.

I'm uh in the middle of –

Actually, I've been thinking about creating a digital magazine of art and criticism.

FRANKLIN. Like a blog.

EMILY. Like a digital magazine.

FRANKLIN. That's awesome. You heard about the sudden demise of *The Honolulu Weekly.*

EMILY. And with no alternative independent newspaper, there needs to be a new outlet to inspire local residents to question ourselves.

To question everything and stop being passive observers.

FRANKLIN. You sound like a grant application.

EMILY. Shut up.

FRANKLIN. It's sexy as hell.

EMILY. Oh.

FRANKLIN. So.

EMILY. So.

FRANKLIN. Would you like to try this whole "meeting in real life" thing again?

EMILY. Did you want to go to Doraku?

FRANKLIN. Well, actually I was thinking of La Mariana.

EMILY. Isn't that the restaurant on the pier?

FRANKLIN. Yup.

EMILY. That sounds. Yeah.

FRANKLIN. Friday at eight.

EMILY. Terrif.

FRANKLIN. Alrighty!

(Click.)

Thirty One

(Telephone rings.)

DAD. Hello?

EMILY. Dad.

DAD. Mimi?

EMILY. I'm at the store. Could you measure the living room wall?

DAD. Oh I. Well. Hold on. My new piezoelectric actuator just arrived!

I'm bending voltage into sound!

EMILY. Dad.

DAD. What are you buying?

EMILY. Bookshelves. For our new place. I wanted to get some that could fit all your books and records.

DAD. I was going to leave most of that at the house.

EMILY. Don't you want to have access?

DAD. Well sure, sweetie. Just get whatever you think is best.

EMILY. Dad, I'm really excited about getting this apartment with you dad, it's going to really help me get back on my feet.

DAD. I'm glad, sweetie.

EMILY. I had a good interview with Bill Tapia. He's really charming.

DAD. Oh good.

EMILY. I'm going to be home late tonight. Did you eat dinner?

DAD. I had some crackers. That really filled me up.

EMILY. What about the chili I made?

DAD. I had some for lunch but I didn't feel like eating it cold again.

EMILY. Heat it up.

DAD. There's no microwave.

EMILY. Heat it up on the stove.

DAD. Your mother said we could buy a microwave.

EMILY. I don't want a microwave.

DAD. I thought you didn't want me to use the stove.

EMILY. I want you to use the stove. I just don't want to die in a fiery gas explosion.

Can't you just remember to turn to burner off all the way?

DAD. Your mother kept a note up to remind me.

EMILY. Can't you write a note for yourself?

DAD. I'll buy more sandwiches.

EMILY. Dad, you're driving me crazy.

DAD. That's not a very nice thing to say. I'm not even hungry.

EMILY. I don't understand why you can't just –

DAD. Mm.

(Click. **DAD** *hangs up.)*

EMILY. Did you just hang up on me?

Thirty Two

(Telephone rings.)

EMILY. Hello?

FRANKLIN. I'm driving away from you.

EMILY. I wanted you to come in.

FRANKLIN. What!

You could have asked me up. "For coffee."

EMILY. You could have pretended you needed to use my bathroom. But you didn't.

FRANKLIN. I thought you'd say no. Because you're a lady.

EMILY. I would have said no. Because that's how much of a lady I am.

Also my dads here.

FRANKLIN. Is it too early to ask how the real date compares to the fantasy?

EMILY. The food was awful. But the view.

FRANKLIN. Can't beat a view of the water. Although, I'm sorry, didn't realize –

You're really afraid of birds.

EMILY. I –

I can't remember the last time I watched the sunset over the ocean.

FRANKLIN. Can you believe that happens every single day?

EMILY. Well. Yes. But not that it's always that beautiful.

FRANKLIN. We should watch another one sometime.

EMILY. That's a little cheesy, isn't it?

FRANKLIN. You make me cheesy. You're a good dancer.

EMILY. I am NOT a good dancer.

FRANKLIN. You know how to move those hips.

EMILY. What hips?

FRANKLIN. I like your curves.

EMILY. My mother says I've got an hourglass figure/

> but most of the sand is at
> the bottom.

FRANKLIN. You do/

> Oh. That's not very nice.

EMILY. That's my mother...

FRANKLIN. I think you're a delicious, sensuous woman.

EMILY. Listen to you.

FRANKLIN. I can't believe you're interested in me.

When I realized you were the actress on the radio, I couldn't believe my luck.

EMILY. What?

FRANKLIN. Ah. I'm losing my cool. I never thought Emily Chang would be interested in me.

EMILY. ... We've met before?

FRANKLIN. You don't remember me?

EMILY. I'm sorry. You look a little familiar. But how do I know you?

FRANKLIN. We went to Kaimuki together.

EMILY. *Frankie Anbe?*

FRANKLIN. You wouldn't give me the time of day in high school.

EMILY. That's because you were horrible to me in junior high.

You were horrible.

FRANKLIN. Ahh. That was a long/time ago.

EMILY. You'd sneak up behind me and throw garbage into my backpack – Chicken bones and once Cherry Jell-O that melted all over my algebra textbook. I had to buy a new one.

FRANKLIN. Ye-ah...

EMILY. You and your friends called Landon a fag and when I told you to shut up you shoved me into the dirt.

FRANKLIN. I think I just lightly pushed you and you fell back into the dirt.

EMILY. Is that all you have to say for yourself?

FRANKLIN. I'm sorry?

EMILY. Okay...?

FRANKLIN. I was a raging barrel of hormones at that time. I'm sorry I was awful to you.

I liked you back then. I've always liked you. You had a nice time tonight, with me.

Right? I mean, you said you think I'm sexy.

EMILY. That was before I knew you were my junior high nemesis.

FRANKLIN. I wanted to apologize to you and Landon at the reunion. But when I saw you with your boyfriend, it felt so juvenile so I left. Can't we...move on?

Can't you know me as I am now?

EMILY. I'm sorry, Frankie. I'm sure you're a perfectly decent human adult.

But any sexual attraction I might have had for you just drained out.

FRANKLIN. Maybe if we saw each other again...

EMILY. Why didn't you bring it up sooner? We grew up together, for God's sake.

FRANKLIN. I thought it was something we weren't going to talk about.

You really didn't know it was me? I mean, I know I lost the weight.

EMILY. God. What a disappointment.

FRANKLIN. Now, hold on. Let me at least –

    (Click. **EMILY** *hangs up the phone.)*

Thirty Three

(Telephone rings.)

MRS. ASUNCION. Hello?

EMILY. Good afternoon, my name is Emily, and I'm calling on behalf of the Honolulu Repertory Theater to see if you would be interested in purchasing a subscription package. A subscription package offers the lowest –

MRS. ASUNCION. Emily Chang?

EMILY. Wha-what?

MRS. ASUNCION. Ehh. Dis is Aleta Asuncion. Landon's maddah?

EMILY. Oh! Hi Mrs. Asuncion.

MRS. ASUNCION. Landon wen tell me you was back in town.

You working for HRT now?

EMILY. Only part time while I look for a new gig.

MRS. ASUNCION. I've been meaning for call you.

Landon wen give me your article about da ethics of photography.

EMILY. Yes, Jean Baudrillard believed reality does not exist, there are only pictures.

MRS. ASUNCION. Mm. Yes. Very disturbing.

EMILY. Thank you so much.

MRS. ASUNCION. Eh, you get any ideas for one story for *Da Star-Advertiser?*

EMILY. Oh! I'm almost finished working on an article about Bill Tapia.

MRS. ASUNCION. Dat's perfect. He going have, one concert at da Waikiki Shell for his 104th.

EMILY. I have tickets.

MRS. ASUNCION. I think can fit dis into next week's Friday Arts section.

We going do one big spread with lots of photos of Bill, past and present, okay?

EMILY. Mrs. Asuncion that would be amazing.

MRS. ASUNCION. Wat's your email, I going send you one work-for-hire agreement.

EMILY. It's Emily Chang-ety Chang 99 at gmail dot com.

MRS. ASUNCION. Ey, I wen run into your maddah at da Kapiolani Farmer's Market.

Poor ting her. How she holding up?

EMILY. Uh great. She's doing great – Mrs. Asuncion, I really appreciate this.

MRS. ASUNCION. Eh. You know Emily, you shoula wen send me da article directly.

Why you no write me when you get into town?

EMILY. I know Landon mentioned it but I didn't want to play that card...

MRS. ASUNCION. Emily. You need to play all da cards in your hand. Always.

EMILY. Right. No. Absolutely. You're right. Thank you.

MRS. ASUNCION. My pleasure. Take care Emily.

EMILY. Oh wait. Uh. Did you want to buy a subscription?

MRS. ASUNCION. Absolutely not.

EMILY. Okay great! No problem! Take care! Thank you again!

(Click.)

Thirty Four

(Telephone rings.)

HALIMA. Hi you've reached Halima. *(Sound of children laughing.)*

Please leave a message and I'll call you back when I can!

(Beep.)

EMILY. Halima.

Those fake journal entries are harsh and kind of dangerous.

I think you are destroying a pretty decent marriage.

If you want to divorce him, okay.

But do you need to torture him?

I know I'm raw about this whole topic anyway.

But...

You have kids, and I don't know.

I'm starting to think there aren't a lot of great guys out there, and maybe Nigel is one of them?

Just a thought. Love you.

(Beep.)

Thirty Five

(Sounds of typing. Tape rewinding. Tape plays. Sounds of typing.)

EMILY. Okay Bill. Are you ready for my next question?

*(**EMILY** winces at the sound of her own voice.)*

BILL. You go ahead honey.

EMILY. How does it feel to be the world's oldest entertainer?

BILL. Who's old?

EMILY. I heard you taught Clark Gable, Rita Hayworth, and Shirley Temple how to play the ukulele.

BILL. Oh yeah. Shirley was da best student.

EMILY. Who else did you play with?

BILL. Oh just about everybady. Bing Crosby and Louie Armstrong.

One night Elvis Presley, and den King Bennie Nawahi. –

*(**EMILY** pauses. She rewinds the tape. She types.)*

– Presley, and den King Bennie Nawahi. He was da real king. You know him?

EMILY. I'm afraid I don't.

(Sound of swallowing.)

You alright?

BILL. I'm just grand honey. I have trouble swallowing pills. I broke mah arm.

EMILY. Are you okay?

BILL. You better believe! I practice every day. A little here 'n' dere. You play?

EMILY. I'm afraid I don't. But my father knows everything about music.

BILL. But not how to play? Ah. Dat's no good. Everybady should play someting.

I learned to play when I was seven-years-old till now. Dat's one long time!

EMILY. That really is.

BILL. How old you?

EMILY. I'm twenty nine.

BILL. Oh too bad baby. You too old for me. You gotta find anaddah fella.

EMILY. I'm working on that.

BILL. My wife Barbie, she wen undastand dat music was my life and she'd come on tour and she'd sing "To You My Sweetheart Aloha."

I had a good wife.

She kept me off da dope and da booze. She was all I needed.

I was married for seventy-tree years. You'd think dat's enough.

But I still talk to her everyday.

I say.

Chee. Barbie. You was one very, very good cook and a nice person and I love you.

When I wen check on you when you was sick. I said,

"It's me, Tappy, it's time to take you pills."

But you no say noting.

I said, "Chee baby why you smiling?"

And that's wen I knew, you was gone.

…

Who am I talking to?

Who you?

EMILY. Bill, remember, it's Emily.

ALYSSA. Sorry Emily, Bill's a little tired. Can you come back another time?

EMILY. Sure. I'm sorry Alyssa. I hope I didn't –

ALYSSA. It's fine. He just needs to –

(**EMILY** *stops the recording.*)

Thirty Six

(Telephone rings.)

LANDON. It's Landon, bitch.

(Beep.)

(BILL *plays a ukulele acoustic version of a song in the style of Bill Tapia's "To You Sweetheart, Aloha".*)*

EMILY. Isn't Bill amazing? You're going to love this article.

By the way, I went on a date with Frankie Two Scoops Anbe. Can you believe it?

(Click.)

---

* A license to produce TODAY IS MY BIRTHDAY does not include a performance license for any third-party or copyrighted music. Licensees should create an original composition or use music in the public domain. For further information, please see the Music and Third-Party Materials Use Note on page iii.

Thirty Seven

(Telephone rings.)

EMILY. Hi, Mrs. Asuncion. I mean Aleta.

MRS. ASUNCION. Emily. So great work on da article.

EMILY. Thanks! Did you get my new lede? I interviewed some of Bills musician friends.

I even got Jake Shimabukuro to –

MRS. ASUNCION. You wen see today's papah?

EMILY. No. Not yet.

MRS. ASUNCION. Here's da ting. Bill Tapia died.

EMILY. Oh no.

His birthday concert is Sunday.

MRS. ASUNCION. I know. It's cancelled now, of course. Dey already ran with da obit they had on file.

So Lehua no like run annada piece on him, yeah.

EMILY. Why didn't they talk to me? I was the last person to interview him.

Didn't they know I was in the middle of revising the article?

MRS. ASUNCION. Obits move fast. Feel free to pitch dis to annada magazine, yeah? It's one good piece.

EMILY. Yeah. Thanks.

MRS. ASUNCION. My maddah wen take me to see Bill play in da '60s at da Royal Hawaiian.

He wen put da uke behind his head. Wow. He was someting. Plenny handsome too.

I know you disappointed. But send me mo' ideas soon, yeah?

EMILY. Oh sure. Yeah. *(Click.)*

Thirty Eight

(Telephone rings.)

LANDON. New Pacific Design –

EMILY. Landon. It's Emily. I just got off the phone with your mom.

LANDON. I heard.

EMILY. Because he's dead, no one cares about him anymore. Now he's joined the ranks of Buddy Holly and Mozart and other artists way more famous than him. It's bullshit.

LANDON. I'm sorry. I know you really loved him.

EMILY. Yeah.

And it's like… I have a Master's degree from Columbia. I have a strong portfolio. Why is it so difficult to get a job here? I mean, it's not like this town is teeming with serious journalists.

LANDON. That's what you think?

EMILY. What? You know I'm right.

LANDON. My maddah was one substitute English teacher for twenty years before she wen work for *The Star Advertiser*. Dat doesn't mean she's not one great editor.

EMILY. Your mom is great, but let's face it. Hawaii isn't on the same level as New York.

LANDON. Hawai'i is fucking awesome and there are fucking awesome things happening here. And I'm tired of you complaining about how provincial it is, just because it's not the big apple.

EMILY. Don't say big apple.

LANDON. When we graduated I watched everybody go away to fancy mainland colleges, while I stayed behind. If you're shiny and ambitious, you leave.

EMILY. I came back.

LANDON. And now were supposed to be grateful that you're back slumming it island-style?

EMILY. God Landon, I'm just venting.

LANDON. No. This is clearly what you believe.

EMILY. I worked hard to get off this rock. Why are you overreacting?

LANDON. Listening to you makes me question my accomplishments because they didn't happen in New York. Nothing's good enough for you here.

EMILY. None of this is a criticism of you.

LANDON. I should get back to work.

(Click.)

Thirty Nine

(Telephone rings.)

HALMIA. Hey Island Girl.

EMILY. Hey City Girl.

So how's the gate working?

HALIMA. The gate keeps Layla from leaving her room when she sleepwalks, so that's a relief.

It's weird though, I mean, its a dog gate.

EMILY. As long as it gives you peace of mind.

How's therapy going?

HALIMA. The same.

Well. Nigel went off on one of his rants.

EMILY. The "children are bastards" rant?

HALIMA. And then in the middle of it, he stopped. He started smiling and laughing.

He thanked the therapist. And in the car he said.

"You knew."

"You've never cheated on me a day in your life."

"You knew I had been reading it and you created this elaborate fiction to punish me."

"I love you so much. I'm such an idiot."

EMILY. Thank God it's finally over. What did you say?

HALIMA. I turned to him, without skipping a beat and I said,

"Hold on. You've been reading my diary?"

"How dare you? How dare you invade my personal thoughts?"

"You...you didn't make it up? You didn't know I was reading your journal?"

"How could I?"

And then he dropped me off at the house and drove off. I haven't seen him since.

EMILY. Halima. My dearest friend.

You are turning into the craziest bitch I know.

HALIMA. I knew I shouldn't talk to you about this.

EMILY. What does that mean?

HALIMA. I can't just fly to Hawaii to escape my problems.

EMILY. Excuse me?

HALIMA. I have a children and a mortgage. No matter what I want, there's no way I won't be somehow attached to this man for the rest of my life.

That's what I'm saying. You cannot begin to comprehend what I'm dealing with.

EMILY. Do you think you're better than me?

Because you're married and produced offspring?

My life is falling apart. I am in the *middle* of my parent's divorce.

HALIMA. – They probably stayed together for your sake.

EMILY. I cannot believe you just said that to me.

HALIMA. I bet you haven't even talked to your mom about her side.

EMILY. I don't need to.

HALIMA. I'm glad you aren't taking sides.

(Sound of a door slam.)

EMILY. What was that?

HALIMA. *(Whispering.)*

I have to go.

EMILY. What? I'm not done being mad at you.

HALIMA. He's home.

EMILY. What's going on? Are you going to be okay? He's not going to.

Nigel's not a violent guy. Is he?

HALIMA. Gotta go-bye.

(Click.)

Forty

(Telephone rings.)

HALIMA. Hi you've reached Halima. *(Sound of children laughing.)* Please leave a message and I'll call you back when I can!

(Beep. Sound of fumbled hang up.)

Forty One

(Telephone rings.)

HALIMA. Hi you've reached Halima. *(Sound of children laughing.)* Please leave a message and I'll call you back when I can!

(Beep.)

EMILY. Halima, are you okay? Call me back.

(Click.)

Forty Two

(Telephone rings.)

SEBASTIAN. Hey...

EMILY. Hi Sebastian.

SEBASTIAN. Emily. What's. What's going on?

EMILY. Are you still friends with Nigel?

SEBASTIAN. Nigel... Wallace? Why?

EMILY. I'm worried about him and Halima. They've been having some marital problems, and she's not answering her phone. I know you guys play squash sometimes.

SEBASTIAN. I used to.

EMILY. Can you call him? See what's going on?

SEBASTIAN. I could...

EMILY. But you won't.

SEBASTIAN. I don't feel comfortable doing that.

EMILY. Ask Nigel to lunch. Tell him you need his advice.

SEBASTIAN. Why don't you call her mother? Or her friends?

EMILY. This is a delicate situation.

SEBASTIAN. I don't know what you want me to do.

EMILY. I JUST TOLD YOU WHAT I WANT YOU TO DO.

SEBASTIAN. Whoa.

EMILY. I need to know if she's okay.

SEBASTIAN. This is their personal, private life. It's none of my business. And frankly, it's none of yours. Halima is a strong woman. Nige's a good guy. And the bottom line is, they are both grown ups. Maybe you should put your energy towards letting things go.

EMILY. Ex-cuse me?

SEBASTIAN. You're probably worked up about nothing.

EMILY. Letting go of what exactly?

SEBASTIAN. I didn't have to answer the phone when you called.

EMILY. I took the photo you are using on your Bumble* profile. You laughing in the god damn rowboat in Central Park framed by stupid-fucking cherry blossoms.

SEBASTIAN. So what? It's the most flattering picture I had on hand.

How did you find my –

EMILY.	SEBASTIAN.
Do you know how inappropriate that is? You are smiling and gazing lovingly at ME in that picture and you're using it to ensnare other women. Oh. And then you butt dialed me on your DATE.	Ensnare?

SEBASTIAN. … What did you hear?

EMILY. Why? Did you get lucky?

SEBASTIAN. How can you even ask me that?

Yes. I was on a date and its none of your fucking business.

(Beat.)

---

* Please use the most appropriate/timely dating app

Aw. Jesus. Don't cry.

EMILY. Just because I didn't say anything doesn't mean I'm crying, asshole.

SEBASTIAN. I know you.

EMILY. You used to know me.

SEBASTIAN. I know you.

And you're the one calling me in the middle of the night, talking about how you met some great guy. This Keoni dude. How do you think that makes me feel?

EMILY. I got hit by a car!

SEBASTIAN. What?

EMILY. Never mind –

How could you break up with me via text message?

SEBASTIAN. You were the one moving your stuff out of the apartment.

EMILY. I needed space. I didn't want to break up.

SEBASTIAN. That's not what it looked like. I thought we could have moved past it.

Lots of couples have miscarriages –

EMILY. I don't want to talk about that. And it wasn't even a fucking –

Never mind. Fuck. Fuck you.

SEBASTIAN. Maybe I overreacted.

Things felt so broken and I felt so guilty for what you were going through.

It's not that I don't love you.

EMILY. You're speaking in the present tense.

SEBASTIAN. Force of habit.

EMILY. Ah.

...

I should go. Will you call Nigel?

SEBASTIAN. I'm not wild about that idea. Let me think about it.

EMILY. Thanks for nothing.

SEBASTIAN. What did you just say?

EMILY. I need you to do this for me.

SEBASTIAN. I already told you. I'll think about it.

(Click.)

Forty Three

(Sad wallowing music in background.*)

(Phone dialing.)

(Eight Cups of Tea Intro. Recorded message.)

WOMAN'S VOICE. Romantic breakups are tough. Eight Cups of Tea Listeners value the opportunity to journey with you toward a mended heart. Chatting with your listener is simple, like drinking tea with a trusted friend. Press one to connect with a listener for eighteen and over. Press two, if you are a teen.

(Beep.)

AMAZINGPRESENCE83. Hello. This is AmazingPresence83. I'm so glad you found me.

How can I help you reach contentment?

EMILY. You probably can't.

AMAZINGPRESENCE83. I can listen.

EMILY. Thank you.

AMAZINGPRESENCE83. What do you want to talk about?

EMILY. I just talked to my ex. And I'm sad. There's no one I can talk to right now.

AMAZINGPRESENCE83. What is your good name?

EMILY. Iris.

---

* A license to produce TODAY IS MY BIRTHDAY does not include a performance license for any third-party or copyrighted music. Licensees should create an original composition or use music in the public domain. For further information, please see the Music and Third-Party Materials Use Note on page iii.

AMAZINGPRESENCE83. Iris, are you having suicidal thoughts, Iris?

EMILY. Just regular sad.

AMAZINGPRESENCE83. Happiness is a choice, not an achievement.

Nothing will make you happy until you decide to be happy.

EMILY. Are you reading that off of a poster?

AMAZINGPRESENCE83. *(Gentle laughter.)* It might seem like an oversimplification.

But that is only because it's true. Would you like to talk about your ex?

EMILY. No.

AMAZINGPRESENCE83. So tell me something good.

EMILY. I don't know. I used to know an amazing old man, a musician. He just died.

Today would have been his 104th birthday.

AMAZINGPRESENCE83. Mm. I'm so sorry for your loss.

EMILY. His claim to fame was that he was living history. But now I can't get my article published because no one cares about him anymore.

AMAZINGPRESENCE83. You care.

EMILY. Yeah...well.

AMAZINGPRESENCE83. Iris, you have a very sympathetic voice.

EMILY. Thank you.

AMAZINGPRESENCE83. It makes me feel less sad listening to it.

EMILY. Thank you.

Are you sad too?

AMAZINGPRESENCE83. I'm very sad.

EMILY. I'm sorry.

AMAZINGPRESENCE83. May I ask you just one question?

EMILY. Uh. Okay.

AMAZINGPRESENCE83. Can you describe what you are wearing on your feet?

EMILY. I'm uh. I'm wearing socks?

AMAZINGPRESENCE83. Are your toenails painted?

EMILY. Pink?

AMAZINGPRESENCE83. That's nice. Could I ask you to take your socks off?

EMILY. Are you for real?

AMAZINGPRESENCE83. HAVE YOU TAKEN YOUR SOCKS OFF FOR ME?

EMILY. What kind of help line is this?

> (**AMAZINGPRESENCE83** *emits a low moan. Click.*)

Forty Four

(*Telephone rings.*)

HALIMA. Hi you've reached Halima. (*Sound of children laughing.*) Please leave a message and I'll call you back when I can!

(*Beep.*)

EMILY. Halima, if you don't let me know how you are doing I'm calling the police.

(*Click.*)

(*Telephone rings.*)

HALIMA. Hi you've reached Halima. (Sound of children laughing.) Please leave a message and I'll call you back when I can!

(*Beep.*)

GENERIC FEMALE VOICE. The mailbox is full and cannot accept any messages at this time, goodbye.

(*Click.*)

#

(*Telephone rings.*)

HALIMA. Hi you've reached Halima. (*Sound of children laughing.*) Please leave a message and I'll call you back when I can!

(*Beep.*)

EMILY. Halima –

(*Call waiting sound.*)

Halima. Hey.

HALIMA. *(Whispering.)* Hey, you just called?

EMILY. Are you okay? Tell me you're you okay?

HALIMA. *(Whispering.)* Hey, it's a really bad time, can I call you back?

EMILY. What's wrong?

HALIMA. I'm fine. My book club is about to start.

EMILY. You fucking asshole. You scared the shit out of me.

HALIMA. Sorry. I've been really busy. I'll –

    (Click. **EMILY** *hangs up.)*

Forty Five

(*Telephone rings.*)

DAD. (*Whispering.*) Hello.

EMILY. Dad.

DAD. (*Whispering.*) Mimi?

EMILY. Yes. I just got home, the house is disgusting. Where are you?

> (*A song in the style of "The Consolidated Theatre Hawaii trailer" plays in the background.*)

DAD. (*Whispering.*) They're showing *As I Was Moving Ahead Occasionally I Saw Brief Glimpses of Beauty* on the big screen here for the first time.

EMILY. You went out?

DAD. I'm out with Patsy.

EMILY. I can't hear you.

DAD. Hold on I'm. (*Shuffling. Muffled conversation with Patsy. Normal voice.*)

Hi can you hear me?

EMILY. Yes.

DAD. I'm out with Patsy.

EMILY. Who?

DAD. She's the digital archivist.

---

* A license to produce TODAY IS MY BIRTHDAY does not include a performance license for any third-party or copyrighted music. Licensees should create an original composition or use music in the public domain. For further information, please see the Music and Third-Party Materials Use Note on page iii.

EMILY. The one with the earrings?

DAD. Yes, she makes her own earrings.

EMILY. They're very unique. Isn't she widowed?

DAD. Freddy died six years ago. Wow. Time flies.

EMILY. Are you on a date? I think it's a little soon for that.

DAD. If an intelligent, stylish, and attractive colleague wants to take me to the cinema, I don't think it's the end of the world, do you?

EMILY. She's not stylish.

DAD. Be kind.

EMILY. So. I bought a whiteboard with a list of twenty weekly tasks.

DAD. Can we discuss this later?

EMILY. I'm sorry. But I can't see the dining room table and it's grossing me out.

DAD. You know, I'm happy to support you but I am paying the entire rent.

EMILY. I am grateful. Extremely grateful. But this is about respecting your living environment. Mom got tired of taking care of you and it'd be good for you to learn –

DAD. You think I need this from you? I get it from your mother and now you?

I was really looking forward to this film. And now I'm all stressed out.

EMILY. Dad. I was just trying to teach you…

DAD. You don't need to teach me anything.

Worry about your own problems and stop trying to fix mine.

(Click.)

Forty Six

(Telephone rings.)

TROY. Hello?

EMILY. Hey Troy.

TROY. Hi! Who is this?

EMILY. It's Emily. Chang.

TROY. Whoa.

EMILY. Is this too random?

TROY. It's okay. How are you? How's New York?

EMILY. Well. I'm back home actually.

TROY. Really? You?

EMILY. Yeah...for now.

Do you ever come back?

TROY. Nah. My parents moved away when they retired.

EMILY. That's too bad.

TROY. I miss Hawai'i. I went to Maui on my honeymoon though.

EMILY. Oh. Congratulations.

Who's the lucky lady?

TROY. JiYun. She's an anesthesiologist.

EMILY. Wow. She's the one...

TROY. Yeah. After you.

EMILY. Thats so great!

And you've achieved the fantasy of every Asian mother by marrying a doctor.

TROY. True.

EMILY. Anyway. I was calling because I'm starting up an online publication.

TROY. Nice! Although I don't know if you'd want my advice.

Hypernia Magazine's on an indefinite hiatus.

EMILY. Oh no!

TROY. Too much work. Didn't have your drive.

EMILY. Mmm.

TROY. I'm at the *Chronicle*. I dig it.

(*Text sound.*)

Sorry to be abrupt, but I have to pick up my daughter.

But send me your questions and I'll try to help.

EMILY. A daughter!

TROY. Can you believe it? Hazel is twenty-one months.

EMILY. Whoa! That is SUCH a good age.

TROY. It really is, you know?

EMILY. Well, I won't keep you.

...

TROY. You okay?

EMILY. Yeah. Of course!

I found this shoebox full of all the letters you wrote me.

TROY. Oh wow.

EMILY. I'm looking at a photo of you with floppy 90's Hugh Grant hair.

TROY. I bet I had a lot more of it.

EMILY. You don't have hair?

TROY. I mean. I have some hair.

EMILY. Do you ever look at my letters?

TROY. When you broke up with me, I threw them out.

EMILY. You threw out all of my letters?

TROY. Yeah. In my defense, you had just broken my heart.

EMILY. I'm sorry.

I just.

I know this is weird.

When we were together, you always seemed so content.

But. I.

Can you help me understand what made you so sure about me back then?

How were you able to make that kind of decision so early?

TROY. I was young. I mean. I was wrong.

EMILY. ...

What if you weren't...wrong.

What if it was just me?

TROY. I couldn't say.

EMILY. How did you do it?

TROY. Do what?

EMILY. Your life?

TROY. I don't know what kind of advice you're looking for, but I don't think I can give it to you.

EMILY. I shouldn't have called. I'm sorry.

TROY. I'm glad to hear from you. And about what you're creating in Hawai'i.

EMILY. Actually, I was thinking of moving to San Francisco.

It's too hard to make anything here. Nobody gets what I'm trying to do.

TROY. Really?

EMILY. Living here is so different than coming back for a visit.

TROY. I can imagine. Well. San Francisco would love to have you.

EMILY. Rents pretty crazy huh?

TROY. Oh my God. You are not good at picking affordable cities.

EMILY. I'm not good at picking anything.

TROY. Hey. Easy now. You're talking about my friend.

EMILY. Am I your friend?

TROY. Of course.

(Different ringing sound.)

EMILY. Oh shit. Sorry I Facetimed you with my big fat cheek. Hi.

TROY. Hi stranger.

EMILY. You did lose some hair.

TROY. You should see my dad gut.

EMILY. Show me – Oh come on, that's barely a tummy.

TROY. I really do have to go, but if you end up moving here, let me know, okay?

I think you'll do well wherever you end up living.

EMILY. Thank you, Troy. Really.

TROY. Anytime.

(Click.)

Forty Seven

(The end of a song. Z 101.3 late night intro.
EMILY *is packing a suitcase.)*

DJ SOLANGE. This is DJ Solange filling in for DJ 2-Finga-Poi bringing you Z 101.3 Late Night Advice

Hour with Goddess Sweet Leilani.

(GODDESS SWEET LEILANI *sound cue.)*

GODDESS SWEET LEILANI. Namaste. And we're back with Franklin who is trying to win back his lady love whom he bullied in high school.

FRANKLIN. Junior High.

EMILY. *(Listening to radio.)* What?

DJ SOLANGE. We've asked our Z 101.3 listeners to weigh-in. And here's what Twitter user @Jadedheart808 had to say.

@JADEDHEART808. U decided 2 be the bully now U have 2 face the consequences

A boy was mean to me in the 9th grade & now that I'm in the 11th

I let him know he'll never have a chance with me

If U want the butterfly then U better be nice 2 the caterpillar

#onlyinHawaii #ZHotspot #butterfly

FRANKLIN. I've changed. Doesn't anyone out there believe a person can change?

GODDESS SWEET LEILANI. And the people have spoken. So sorry Franklin. Better luck next time.

*(***GODDESS SWEET LEILANI*** Rejection sound cue.)*

Our next caller is from –

Forty Eight

(A '90s hit plays. Telephone rings.)*

DJ SOLANGE. *(Normal person voice.)* Hello?

EMILY. Hi, I'm trying to reach Goddess Sweet Leilani.

DJ SOLANGE. That program ended. It's ninety songs from the '90s till two.

EMILY. Do you know if that guy that called in, Franklin. Was he an actor or not?

DJ SOLANGE. Why would he be an actor?

EMILY. Oh come on. I've called in as a performer with you guys before.

DJ SOLANGE. Jesus it's you.

EMILY. Can I go on the air? I just want to say something to him.

I did a number on that guy.

DJ SOLANGE. What would you say to him on the radio you couldn't say in person?

EMILY. Aren't you negating the transformative power of your own medium?

I just want to get on for one second.

DJ SOLANGE. Our producer really doesn't want to use you anymore. He sent an email.

EMILY. Could I dedicate a song to him from his friend, Emily?

---

* A license to produce TODAY IS MY BIRTHDAY does not include a performance license for any third-party or copyrighted music. Licensees should create an original composition or use music in the public domain. For further information, please see the Music and Third-Party Materials Use Note on page iii.

DJ SOLANGE. I guess. It needs to be from the '90s.

EMILY. Let me think about it.

Forty Nine

(Telephone rings.)

EMILY. This is Emily. You know what to do.

(Beep.)

MOM.   Emily. Your father says you're moving to San Francisco? Do you have a new job?

Congratulations!

If you don't have a new job, you need at least six months of living expenses saved before you move to a new place.

Please don't leave without saying goodbye.

That's not what we do, Emily.

Okay?

This is your mother.

(Click.)

Fifty

(Telephone rings.)

LANDON. This better be good.

EMILY. Landon please. Please don't be mad at me right now. I'm walking over a highway overpass on Sand Island and I'm really scared.

LANDON. What are you doing there?

EMILY. I was drinking and I hit a telephone pole.

LANDON. What the fuck! You could have killed someone.

EMILY. I know. God. I know.

LANDON. That's really fucked up Emily.

EMILY. I know. It's been a horrific night.

Oh man. *(Lowers voice.)* Up ahead there's a bunch of really sketchy looking dudes.

LANDON. Why don't you wait in your car?

EMILY. I can't be in my car or I'll get a DUI. I have to sort it out in the morning.

LANDON. Can't you get someplace else?

EMILY. There's nothing around here. It's all industrial.

But if I can get to the other side of the overpass there's La Mariana, that restaurant by the pier?

I thought from there I could call a car... or you can get me.

LANDON. Keep talking to me. Keep walking. – *(Offstage.)* You need to leave

– I'll start driving towards you.

EMILY. Shit. Come quick.

If something happens, I'm on Sand Island Access Road.

Just passing this auto recycling center.

LANDON. Jesus, Emily. Are you trying to get murdered?

EMILY. I'm going to get rape-murdered. Oh my God.

LANDON. Calm down.

EMILY. My suitcases are in the trunk. And my laptop.

But I didn't want to carry them down the street.

LANDON. Suitcases?

EMILY. I booked a flight to San Francisco.

LANDON. What the fuck? You were gonna ghost?

EMILY. I need a new city.

LANDON. So you drove yourself drunk to the airport?

EMILY. My flight was delayed. So I went to the airport bar. And then my flight was cancelled.

So I got my car back, and – I'm supposed to fly out again tomorrow.

LANDON. And now?

EMILY. As soon as I sort out my car, I'm out of here.

LANDON. Girl. You're bell-jaring.

EMILY. I'm starting fresh.

LANDON. Nuh-uh.

EMILY. Are you close?

LANDON. I wasn't alone when you called.

EMILY. Oh. Did I.

LANDON. He was leaving.

This married guy I've been seeing brought his baby over.

EMILY. He brought his baby to a hookup?

LANDON. In a fucking baby Björn. When I asked him about it, he said, "don't worry. She won't wake up." He was supposedly driving her around the neighborhood so she'd stop crying and fall asleep, but he came over to see me instead.

EMILY. So you asked him to leave?

LANDON. I mean. The baby was asleep.

EMILY. His poor wife. Can you imagine?

LANDON. Judge me all you want.

EMILY. At least you didn't fool around with your boss.

LANDON. I do have standards.

EMILY. You should know that I didn't come back here to boost myself up because I think I'm better than everyone.

I came here because I failed in every single way.

LANDON. It's painful how negative you are about Hawai'i when I know you love it.

EMILY. I love aspects of Hawai'i. But not myself in it.

LANDON. Not to go all mystical *kupuna* on you.

But it's like *nānā i ke kumu*. Look to your source. Let it energize you.

EMILY. You know that's not going to work.

LANDON. Why not?

EMILY. Can I tell you something?

If you promise not to feel bad for me?

LANDON. Go ahead girl.

EMILY. Well...

I haven't told anyone this before.

When I was with Sebastian, we got pregnant.

It was ectopic, where the egg attaches outside of the uterus.

It's super dangerous and there's only a tiny chance that I'd be able to carry it to term.

I knew I was being crazy and so unbelievably stupid,

but

I couldn't bring myself to take the medication to terminate,

because of that tiny,

sliver of hope.

So there was this life,

growing in the wrong part of my body.

Killing me.

LANDON. Jesus.

EMILY. I didn't tell a soul and went on like everything was normal.

I watched Sebastian child-proof our tiny apartment

and read up about newborns. And I didn't say a thing.

Then I had an abdominal rupture, and I got rushed to the hospital.

I lost the baby.

And now it's pretty unlikely that I can ever get pregnant again.

LANDON. Emily. I'm so – *Sorry*.

EMILY. I just want to do something that matters, you know?

When I was little, my dad used to read me this book that in retrospect, really fucked me up. *Miss Rumphius?* It's about this girl who's told that when she grows up, she must do something to make the world more beautiful.

What can any of us do to truly make the world more beautiful?

Shit.

Hold on. There's a sketchy car flashing its lights at me.

LANDON. That's your white knight in a used Kia Optima.

I'm here!

We're getting some mother-fucking loco moco and macadamia nut pancakes.

You'll feel better, you fucking lush.

EMILY. Thank you.

Fifty One

MOM. Chang residence, you've reached Grace.

EMILY. Is it still the Chang residence if you are living by yourself?

MOM. It's debatable. Could that be my daughter?

EMILY. Hi mom.

Did you get the articles I sent you?

MOM. I don't much care about the plight of downtown graffiti "artists," but I thought it was well-written. And I loved the piece about Bill.

EMILY. Thanks.

MOM. So are you and Landon writing *every* article in the magazine?

EMILY. Come on, we have to start somewhere.

MOM. You don't need to assume everything I say is a criticism.

Have you talked to your father?

EMILY. He's been spending time with the Digital Archivist, Patsy.

MOM. I know. She made me buy a pair of her earrings.

EMILY. Doesn't it bother you?

MOM. Should it?

EMILY. It bothers me. Are you still going through with the divorce?

MOM. I'm doing really well right now. I started taking a Zumba class with Aunty Feng Feng.

EMILY. Don't you miss dad?

MOM. I talk to your father every day.

I think he's still hurt that you moved out.

EMILY. I don't know how you did it, mom.

What if he ends up with that Patsy woman?

MOM. It's possible. Men tend to remarry more than women.

EMILY. That's so messed up. Because men are supposedly better looking when they're older?

MOM. There was an article I was thinking about sending you but decided against it.

It was career advice from the director Stanley Kubrick.

You know he directed *The Shining* and *2001/A Space Odyssey.*

EMILY. I know who Stanley Kubrick is.

MOM. Kubrick talked about how his wife supported him and maintained the household, and basically took care of him in all kinds of ways throughout his career. But for the female artists he knows, they get caught up by taking care of their children and husbands, and marriage becomes detrimental to their careers.

So his advice for men is: "get married."

And his advice to women is: "Don't get married. Stay single and stop taking care of men."

EMILY. This is your advice to me?

MOM. This is my advice to myself.

EMILY. What are you doing right now?

MOM. Nothing.

EMILY. Wanna get dim sum?

MOM. Not really. Come with me to Macys, I have to do returns.

EMILY. ...yeah, okay.

Fifty Two

(Public radio intro music.*)

JOYCE. *Aloha kakahiaka.* This is Joyce Young for *Island Chat* for Hawai'i Public Radio 88.1 FM. My guest today is Emily Chang, founder of *The Outpost,* a digital magazine of art and criticism. The theme in this issue is magical thinking in various forms, and features articles by local and national writers. How are you today, Emily?

EMILY. Really well. Thank you Joyce.

JOYCE. You sound very calm. Do you have prior experience on the radio?

EMILY. Actually...yes.

JOYCE. So I love the magazine and it's been having a huge impact. *Wired Magazine* names *The Outpost* one of the best new independent magazines you've never heard of.

In this piece called "The Plight of the Alone," you've written, can you please read this wonderful passage for our listeners?

EMILY. Oh. Okay. "We need each other now more than ever. In a world where communication is effortlessly impersonal, an insistence on independence can be dangerous. Our essential needs haven't altered over time – there's no app to erase our need to breathe, sleep, and eat. But overlaying our essential needs is a map of desire. All of us are alone, but we need to appreciate our dependence. We are made up of thousands of others."

JOYCE. Mmm. At the end of the day, whether you're an extrovert, or an introvert, like me, surprise! All humans experience loneliness.

And what do you need most?

EMILY. What or who?

JOYCE. You tell me.

Can you respond to that

Tell me more

But what do we do about it

End of Play

www.ingramcontent.com/pod-product-compliance
Lightning Source LLC
Chambersburg PA
CBHW070329120726
47909CB00008B/2656